ERNEST HEMINGWAY

The Old Man and the Sea

Edited by Paul Kämmer
Explanatory notes by Ingrid Jacob

W0333462

Hueber

The Old Man and the Sea was originally published in 1952
by Charles Scribner's Sons, New York.
The present abridged school edition is the only one authorized
in Germany.

Das Werk und seine Teile sind urheberrechtlich geschützt. Jede Verwertung in anderen als den gesetzlich zugelassenen Fällen bedarf deshalb der vorherigen schriftlichen Einwilligung des Verlags.

12. 11. | Die letzten Ziffern
2003 02 01 | bezeichnen Zahl und Jahr des Druckes.
Alle Drucke dieser Auflage können, da unverändert,
nebeneinander benutzt werden.
24. Auflage 1977
© 1960 Max Hueber Verlag, D-85737 Ismaning
Umschlagzeichnung: Erich Hölle, Otterfing
Druck: Ludwig Auer GmbH, Donauwörth
Printed in Germany
ISBN 3-19-000150-2

INTRODUCTION

Ernest Hemingway is one of the greatest American authors of our time. He was born the son of a doctor in a suburb of Chicago in 1899, and was educated at public schools. Even as a young man he showed a noticeable talent for writing, and at the age of sixteen he became a junior reporter for a Kansas newspaper. However, his journalistic career was interrupted by the First World War, in which he served in France and Italy as an ambulance driver. After the war he stayed in Europe working as a foreign correspondent for a Toronto newspaper. In Paris he met Ezra Pound, James Joyce and Gertrude Stein, who stimulated his dedication to literary work. It is in this period that his first novels were published. Nevertheless, since he was an adventurous and daring man, the offer of working as a foreign correspondent in Spain during the Civil War enticed him to return to his old profession and took him to the country which was to be so influential on his writing. Here and in Cuba he became devoted to bull fighting, big-game hunting and deep-sea fishing—sports which are a recurrent theme in his subsequent short stories and novels. Ernest Hemingway died in 1961.

His many novels, which reflect his love of nature and sports (hunting, boxing, bull fighting) and give evidence of his deep understanding of the human soul, include such famous works as *The Sun Also Rises* (1926), *A Farewell to Arms* (1929), and *For Whom the Bell Tolls* (1940). In addition he wrote several volumes of short stories and also a play.

The Old Man and the Sea, published in 1952, is regarded by many as the finest work Hemingway ever wrote. The simplicity of form and the avoidance of sentimentality displayed here are typical of Hemingway, who is merely relating the episodes as a reporter would do. His crisp, matter-of-fact style which can be seen in his treatment of the friendship between the old fisherman and the boy gives the book its warmth and reaches great depths of feeling. The choice of subject and the fatalistic attitude which can be felt throughout the story are all characteristic of Hemingway's art and personality. As we witness the toughness and courage of a simple old man in the face of adversity, we are reminded of Hemingway's famous words: "A man can be destroyed but not defeated."

In 1954 Ernest Hemingway was awarded the Nobel Prize for literature for the narrative art displayed in *The Old Man and the Sea.*

Paul Kämmer

THE OLD MAN AND THE SEA

He was an old man who fished alone in a skiff in the Gulf Stream and he had gone eighty-four days now without taking a fish. In the first forty days a boy had been with him. But after forty days without a fish the boy's parents had told him that the old man was now definitely and finally *salao*, which is the worst form of unluck, and the boy had gone at their orders in another boat which caught three good fish the first week. It made the boy sad to see the old man come in each day with his skiff empty and he always went down to help him carry either the coiled lines or the gaff and harpoon and the sail that was furled around the mast. The sail was patched with flour sacks and, furled, it looked like the flag of permanent defeat.

The old man was thin and gaunt with deep wrinkles in the back of his neck. The brown blotches of the benevolent skin cancer the sun brings from its reflection on the tropic sea were on his cheeks. The blotches ran well down the sides of his face and his hands had the deep-creased scars from handling heavy fish on the cords. But none of these scars were fresh. They were as old as erosions in a fishless desert.

Everything about him was old except his eyes and they were the same colour as the sea and were cheerful and undefeated.

"Santiago," the boy said to him as they climbed the bank from where the skiff was hauled up. "I could go with you again. We've made some money."

The old man had taught the boy to fish and the boy loved him.

"No," the old man said. "You're with a lucky boat. Stay with them."

"But remember how you went eighty-seven days without fish and then we caught big ones every day for three weeks."

"I remember," the old man said. "I know you did not leave me because you doubted."

"It was papa who made me leave. I am a boy and I must obey him."

"I know," the old man said. "It is quite normal."

They walked up the road together to the old man's shack and went in through its open door. The old man leaned the mast with its wrapped sail against the wall and the boy put the box and the other gear beside it. The mast was nearly as long as the one room of the shack. The shack was made of the tough bud-shields of the royal palm which are called *guano* and in it there was a bed, a table, one chair, and a place on the dirt floor to cook with charcoal. On the brown walls of the flattened, overlapping leaves of the sturdy fibred *guano* there was a picture in colour of the Sacred Heart of Jesus and another of the Virgin of Cobre. These were relics of his wife. Once there had been a tinted photograph of his wife on the wall but he had taken it down because it made him too lonely to see it and it was on the shelf in the corner under his clean shirt.

"What do you have to eat?" the boy asked.

"A pot of yellow rice with fish. Do you want some?"

"No. I will eat at home. Do you want me to make the fire?"

"No. I will make it later on. Or I may eat the rice cold."

"May I take the cast net?"

"Of course."

There was no cast net and the boy remembered when they had sold it. But they went through this fiction every day. There was no pot of yellow rice and fish and the boy knew this too.

"Eighty-five is a lucky number," the old man said. "How would you like to see me bring one in that dressed out over a thousand pounds?"

"I'll get the cast net and go for sardines. Will you sit in the sun in the doorway?"

"Yes. I have yesterday's paper and I will read the baseball."

"You study it and tell me when I come back."

"Do you think we should buy a terminal of the lottery with an eighty-five? Tomorrow is the eighty-fifth day."

"We can do that," the boy said. "But what about the eighty-seven of your great record?"

"It could not happen twice. Do you think you can find an eighty-five?"

"I can order one."

The boy left him there and when he came back the old man was asleep.

"Wake up old man," the boy said and put his hand on one of the old man's knees.

The old man opened his eyes and for a moment he was coming back from a long way away. Then he smiled.

"What have you got?" he asked.

"Supper," said the boy. "We're going to have supper."

"I'm not very hungry."

"Come on and eat. You can't fish and not eat."

"I have," the old man said getting up and taking the newspaper and folding it. Then he started to fold the blanket.

"Keep the blanket around you," the boy said.

"You'll not fish without eating while I'm alive."

"Then live a long time and take care of yourself," the old man said. "What are we eating?"

"Black beans and rice, fried bananas, and some stew."

The boy had brought them in a two-decker metal container from the Terrace.

"Your stew is excellent," the old man said.

"Tell me about the baseball," the boy asked him.

"In the American League it is the Yankees as I said," the old man said happily.

"They lost today," the boy told him.

"That means nothing. The great DiMaggio is himself again."

"They have other men on the team."

"Naturally. But he makes the difference."

"I would like to take the great DiMaggio fishing," the old man said. "They say his father was a fisherman. Maybe he was as poor as we are and would understand."

"The great Sisler's father was never poor and he, the father, was playing in the big leagues when he was my age."

"When I was your age I was before the mast on a square-rigged ship that ran to Africa and I have seen lions on the beaches in the evening."

"I know. You told me."

"Should we talk about Africa or about baseball?"

"Baseball I think," the boy said.

"Who is the greatest manager, really, Luque or Mike Gonzalez?"

"I think they are equal."

"And the best fisherman is you."

"No. I know others better."

"*Qué va*," the boy said. "There are many good fishermen and some great ones. But there is only you."

"Thank you. You make me happy. I hope no fish will come along so great that he will prove us wrong."

"There is no such fish if you are still strong as you say."

"I may not be as strong as I think," the old man said. "But I know many tricks and I have resolution."

"You ought to go to bed now so that you will be fresh in the morning. I will take the things back to the Terrace."

"Good night then. I will wake you in the morning."

"Sleep well old man."

The boy went out. They had eaten with no light on the table and the old man took off his trousers and went to bed in the dark. He rolled his trousers up to make a pillow, putting the newspaper inside them. He rolled himself in the blanket and slept on the other old newspapers that covered the springs of the bed.

He was asleep in a short time and he dreamed of Africa when

he was a boy and the long, golden beaches and the white beaches, so white they hurt your eyes, and the high capes and the great brown mountains. He lived along that coast now every night and in his dreams he heard the surf roar and saw the native boats come riding through it. He smelled the tar and oakum of the deck as he slept and he smelled the smell of Africa that the land breeze brought at morning.

He no longer dreamed of storms, nor of women, nor of great occurrences, nor of great fish, nor fights, nor contests of strength, nor of his wife. He only dreamed of places now and of the lions on the beach. They played like young cats in the dusk and he loved them as he loved the boy. He never dreamed about the boy. He simply woke, looked out the open door at the moon and unrolled his trousers and put them on. He urinated outside the shack and then went up the road to wake the boy.

The door of the house where the boy lived was unlocked and he opened it and walked in quietly with his bare feet. The boy was asleep on a cot in the first room and the old man could see him clearly with the light that came in from the dying moon. He took hold of one foot gently and held it until the boy woke and turned and looked at him. The old man nodded and the boy took his trousers from the chair by the bed and, sitting on the bed, pulled them on.

The old man went out the door and the boy came after him. He was sleepy and the old man put his arm across his shoulders and said, "I am sorry."

"*Qué va,*" the boy said. "It is what a man must do."

They walked down the road to the old man's shack and all along the road, in the dark, barefoot men were moving, carrying the masts of their boats.

When they reached the old man's shack the boy took the rolls of line in the basket and the harpoon and gaff and the old man carried the mast with the furled sail on his shoulder.

"Do you want coffee?" the boy asked.

"We'll put the gear in the boat and then get some."

They had coffee from condensed-milk cans at an early morning place that served fishermen.

"How did you sleep old man?" the boy asked. He was waking up now although it was still hard for him to leave his sleep.

"Very well, Manolin," the old man said. "I feel confident today."

"So do I," the boy said. "Now I must get your sardines and mine and your fresh baits. He brings our gear himself. He never wants anyone to carry anything."

"We're different," the old man said. "I let you carry things when you were five years old."

"I know it," the boy said. "I'll be right back. Have another coffee. We have credit here."

He walked off, barefooted on the coral rocks, to the ice house where the baits were stored.

The old man drank his coffee slowly. It was all he would have all day and he knew that he should take it. For a long time now eating had bored him and he never carried a lunch. He had a bottle of water in the bow of the skiff and that was all he needed for the day.

The boy was back now with the sardines and the two baits wrapped in a newspaper and they went down the trail to the skiff, feeling the pebbled sand under their feet, and lifted the skiff and slid her into the water.

"Good luck old man."

"Good luck," the old man said. He fitted the rope lashings of the oars onto the thole pins and, leaning forward against the thrust of the blades in the water, he began to row out of the harbour in the dark. There were other boats from the other beaches going out to sea and the old man heard the dip and push of their oars even though he could not see them now the moon was below the hills.

Sometimes someone would speak in a boat. But most of the boats were silent except for the dip of the oars. They spread apart after they were out of the mouth of the harbour and each one headed for the part of the ocean where he hoped to find fish. The old man knew he was going far out and he left the smell of the land behind and rowed out into the clean early morning smell of the ocean.

In the dark the old man could feel the morning coming and as he rowed he heard the trembling sound as flying fish left the water and the hissing that their stiff set wings made as they soared away in the darkness. He was very fond of flying fish as they were his principal friends on the ocean. He was sorry for the birds, especially the small delicate dark terns that were always flying and looking and almost never finding, and he thought, "The birds have a harder life than we do except for the robber birds and the heavy strong ones. Why did they make birds so delicate and fine as those sea swallows when the ocean can be so cruel? She is kind and very beautiful. But she can be so cruel and it comes so suddenly and such birds that fly, dipping and hunting, with their small sad voices are made too delicately for the sea."

He was rowing steadily and it was no effort for him since he kept well within his speed and the surface of the ocean was flat except for the occasional swirls of the current. He was letting the current do a third of the work and as it started to be light he saw he was already further out than he had hoped to be at this hour.

I worked the deep wells for a week and did nothing, he thought. Today I'll work out where the schools of bonita and albacore are and maybe there will be a big one with them.

Before it was really light he had his baits out and was drifting with the current. One bait was down forty fathoms. The second was at seventy-five and the third and fourth were down in the blue water at one hundred and one hundred and twenty-five fathoms. Each bait hung head down with the shank of the hook inside the bait fish, tied and sewed solid, and all the projecting part of the hook, the curve and the point, was covered with fresh sardines. Each sardine was hooked through both eyes so that they made a half-garland on the projecting steel. There was no part of the hook that a great fish could feel which was not sweet-smelling and good-tasting.

Now the man watched the dip of the three sticks over the side of the skiff and rowed gently to keep the lines straight up and down and at their proper depths. It was quite light and any moment now the sun would rise . . .

The sun was two hours higher now and it did not hurt his eyes so much to look into the east. There were only three boats in sight now and they showed very low and far inshore.

All my life the early sun has hurt my eyes, he thought. Yet they are still good. In the evening I can look straight into it without getting the blackness. It has more force in the evening too. But in the morning it is painful.

The clouds over the land now rose like mountains and the coast was only a long green line with the grey-blue hills behind it. The water was a dark blue now, so dark that it was almost purple. As he looked down into it he saw the red sifting of the plankton in the dark water and the strange light the sun made now. He watched his lines to see them go straight down out of sight into the water and he was happy to see so much plankton because it meant fish.

Just then the stern line came taut under his foot, where he had kept a loop of the line, and he dropped his oars and felt the weight of the small tuna's shivering pull as he held the line firm and commenced to haul it in. The shivering increased as he pulled in and he could see the blue back of the fish in the water and the gold of his sides before he swung him over the side and into the boat. He lay in the stern in the sun, compact and bullet-shaped, his big, unintelligent eyes staring as he thumped his life out against the planking of the boat with the quick shivering strokes of his neat, fast-moving tail. The old man hit him on the head for kindness and kicked him, his body still shuddering, under the shade of the stern.

"Albacore," he said aloud. "He'll make a beautiful bait. He'll weigh ten pounds."

He did not remember when he had first started to talk aloud when he was by himself. He had sung when he was by himself in the old days and he had sung at night sometimes when he was alone steerings on his watch in the smacks or in the turtle boats. He had probably started to talk aloud, when alone, when the boy had left. But he did not remember.

The sun was hot now and the old man felt it on the back of his neck and felt the sweat trickle down his back as he rowed.

I could just drift, he thought, and sleep and put a bight of line around my toe to wake me. But today is eighty-five days and I should fish the day well.

Just then, watching his lines, he saw one of the projecting green sticks dip sharply.

"Yes," he said. "Yes," and shipped his oars without bumping the boat. He reached out for the line and held it softly between the thumb and forefinger of his right hand. He felt no strain nor weight and he held the line lightly. Then it came again. This time it was a tentative pull, not solid nor heavy, and he knew exactly what it was. One hundred fathoms down a marlin was eating the sardines that covered the point and the shank of the hook where the hand-forged hook projected from the head of the small tuna.

The old man held the line delicately, and softly, with his left hand, unleashed it from the stick. Now he could let it run through his fingers without the fish feeling any tension.

This far out, he must be huge in this month, he thought. Eat them, fish. Eat them. Please eat them. How fresh they are and you down there six hundred feet in that cold water in the dark. Make another turn in the dark and come back and eat them.

He felt the light delicate pulling and then a harder pull when a sardine's head must have been more difficult to break from the hook. Then there was nothing.

"Come on," the old man said aloud. "Make another turn.

Just smell them. Aren't they lovely? Eat them good now and then there is the tuna. Hard and cold and lovely. Don't be shy, fish. Eat them."

He waited with the line between his thumb and his finger, watching it and the other lines at the same time for the fish might have swum up or down. Then came the same delicate pulling touch again.

"He'll take it," the old man said aloud. "God help him to take it."

He did not take it though. He was gone and the old man felt nothing.

"He can't have gone," he said. "Christ knows he can't have gone. He's making a turn. Maybe he has been hooked before and he remembers something of it."

Then he felt the gentle touch on the line and he was happy.

"It was only his turn," he said. "He'll take it."

He was happy feeling the gentle pulling and then he felt something hard and unbelievably heavy. It was the weight of the fish and he let the line slip down, down, down, unrolling off the first of the two reserve coils. As it went down, slipping lightly through the old man's fingers, he still could feel the great weight, though the pressure of his thumb and finger were almost imperceptible.

"What a fish," he said. "He has it sideways in his mouth now and he is moving off with it."

Then he will turn and swallow it, he thought. He did not say that because he knew that if you said a good thing it might not happen. He knew what a huge fish this was and he thought of him moving away in the darkness with the tuna held crosswise in his mouth. At that moment he felt him stop moving but the weight was still there. Then the weight increased and he gave more line. He tightened the pressure of his thumb and finger for a moment and the weight increased and was going straight down.

"He's taken it," he said. "Now I'll let him eat it well."

He let the line slip through his fingers while he reached down with his left hand and made fast the free end of the two reserve coils to the loop of the two reserve coils of the next line. Now he was ready. He had three forty-fathom coils of line in reserve now, as well as the coil he was using.

"Eat it a little more," he said. "Eat it well."

Eat it so that the point of the hook goes into your heart and kills you, he thought. Come up easy and let me put the harpoon into you. All right. Are you ready? Have you been long enough at table?

"Now!" he said aloud and struck hard with both hands, gained a yard of line and then struck again and again, swinging with each arm alternately on the cord with all the strength of his arms and the pivoted weight of his body.

Nothing happened. The fish just moved away slowly and the old man could not raise him an inch. His line was strong and made for heavy fish and he held it against his back until it was so taut that beads of water were jumping from it. Then it began to make a slow hissing sound in the water and he still held it, bracing himself against the thwart and leaning back against the pull. The boat began to move slowly off toward the north-west.

The fish moved steadily and they travelled slowly on the calm water. The other baits were still in the water but there was nothing to be done.

"I wish I had the boy," the old man said aloud. "I'm being towed by a fish and I'm the towing bitt. I could make the line fast. But then he could break it. I must hold him all I can and give him line when he must have it. Thank God he is travelling and not going down."

What I will do if he decides to go down, I don't know. What I'll do if he sounds and dies I don't know. But I'll do something. There are plenty of things I can do.

He held the line against his back and watched its slant in the water and the skiff moving steadily to the north-west.

This will kill him, the old man thought. He can't do this for ever. But four hours later the fish was still swimming steadily out to sea, towing the skiff, and the old man was still braced solidly with the line across his back.

"It was noon when I hooked him," he said. "And I have never seen him."

Then he looked behind him and saw that no land was visible. That makes no difference, he thought. I can always come in on the glow from Havana. There are two more hours before the sun sets and maybe he will come up before that.

The fish never changed his course nor his direction all that night as far as the man could tell from watching the stars. It was cold after the sun went down and the old man's sweat dried cold on his back and his arms and his old legs. During the day he had taken the sack that covered the bait box and spread it in the sun to dry. After the sun went down he tied it around his neck so that it hung down over his back and he cautiously worked it down under the line that was across his shoulders now. The sack cushioned the line and he had found a way of leaning forward against the bow so that he was almost comfortable. The position actually was only somewhat less intolerable; but he thought of it as almost comfortable.

I can do nothing with him and he can do nothing with me, he thought. Not as long as he keeps this up.

Then he said aloud, "I wish I had the boy. To help me and to see this."

No one should be alone in their old age, he thought. But it is unavoidable. I must remember to eat the tuna before he spoils in order to keep strong. Remember, no matter how little you want to, that you must eat him in the morning. Remember, he said to himself . . .

Then be began to pity the great fish that he had hooked. He is wonderful and strange and who knows how old he is, he thought. Never have I had such a strong fish nor one who acted so strangely. Perhaps he is too wise to jump. He could ruin me by jumping or by a wild rush. But perhaps he has been hooked many times before and he knows that this is how he should make his fight. He cannot know that it is only one man against him, nor that it is an old man. But what a great fish he is and what he will bring in the market if the flesh is good. He took the bait like a male and he pulls like a male and his fight has no panic in it. I wonder if he has any plans or if he is just as desperate as I am?

"I wish the boy was here," he said aloud and settled himself against the rounded planks of the bow and felt the strength of the great fish through the line he held across his shoulders moving steadily toward whatever he had chosen.

When once, through my treachery, it had been necessary to him to make a choice, the old man thought.

His choice had been to stay in the deep dark water far out beyond all snares and traps and treacheries. My choice was to go there to find him beyond all people. Beyond all people in the world. Now we are joined together and have been since noon. And no one to help either one of us.

Perhaps I should not have been a fisherman, he thought. But that was the thing that I was born for. I must surely remember to eat the tuna after it gets light.

Some time before daylight something took one of the baits that were behind him. He heard the stick break and the line begin to rush out over the gunwale of the skiff. In the darkness he loosened his sheath knife and taking all the strain of the fish on his left shoulder he leaned back and cut the line against the wood of the gunwale. Then he cut the other line closest to him and in the dark made the loose ends of the reserve coils fast. He worked skilfully with the one hand and put his foot on the coils to hold them as he drew his knots tight. Now he had six reserve coils of line. There were two from each bait he had severed and the two from the bait the fish had taken and they were all connected.

After it is light, he thought, I will work back to the forty-fathom bait and cut it away too and link up the reserve coils.

I will have lost two hundred fathoms of good Catalan *cordel* and the hooks and leaders. That can be replaced. But who replaces this fish if I hook some fish and it cuts him off? I don't know what that fish was that took the bait just now. It could have been a marlin or a broadbill or a shark. I never felt him. I had to get rid of him too fast.

Aloud he said, "I wish I had the boy."

But you havent't got the boy, he thought. You have only yourself and you had better work back to the last line now, in the dark or not in the dark, and cut it away and hook up the two reserve coils.

So he did it. It was difficult in the dark and once the fish made a surge that pulled him down on his face and made a cut below his eye. The blood ran down his cheek a little way. But it coagulated and dried before it reached his chin and he worked his way back to the bow and rested against the wood. He adjusted the sack and carefully worked the line so that it came across a new part of his shoulders and, holding it anchored with his shoulders, he carefully felt the pull of the fish and then felt with his hand the progress of the skiff through the water.

I wonder what he made that lurch for, he thought. The wire must have slipped on the great hill of his back. Certainly his back cannot feel as badly as mine does. But he cannot pull this skiff for ever, no matter how great he is. Now everything is cleared away that might make trouble and I have a big reserve of line; all that a man can ask.

"Fish," he said softly, aloud, "I'll stay with you until I am dead."

He'll stay with me too, I suppose, the old man thought and he waited for it to be light. It was cold now in the time before daylight and he pushed against the wood to be warm.

When the sun had risen further the old man realized that the fish was not tiring.

Maybe if I can increase the tension just a little it will hurt him and he will jump, he thought. Now that it is daylight let him jump so that he'll fill the sacs along his backbone with air and then he cannot go deep to die.

He tried to increase the tension, but the line had been taut up to the very edge of the breaking point since he had hooked the fish and he felt the harshness as he leaned back to pull and knew he could put no more strain on it. I must not jerk it ever, he thought. Each jerk widens the cut the hook makes and then when he does jump he might throw it. Anyway I feel better with the sun and for once I do not have to look into it.

There was yellow weed on the line but the old man knew that only made an added drag and he was pleased. It was the yellow Gulf weed that had made so much phosphorescence in the night.

"Fish," he said, "I love you and respect you very much. But I will kill you dead before this day ends."

Let us hope so, he thought.

A small bird came toward the skiff from the north. He was a warbler and flying very low over the water. The old man could see that he was very tired. The bird made the stern of the boat and rested there.

Just then the fish gave a sudden lurch that pulled the old man down on to the bow and would have pulled him overboard if he had not braced himself and given some line.

The bird had flown up when the line jerked and the old man had not even seen him go. He felt the line carefully with his right hand and noticed his hand was bleeding.

"Something hurt him then," he said aloud and pulled back on the line to see if he could turn the fish. But when he was touching the breaking point he held steady and settled back against the strain of the line.

"You're feeling it now, fish," he said. "And so, God knows, am I."

He looked around for the bird now because he would have liked him for company. The bird was gone.

You did not stay long, the man thought. But it is rougher where you are going until you make the shore. How did I let the fish cut me with that one quick pull he made? I must be getting very stupid. Or perhaps I was looking at the small bird and thinking of him. Now I will pay attention to my work and then I must eat the tuna so that I will not have a failure of strength.

"I wish the boy were here and that I had some salt," he said aloud.

Shifting the weight of the line to his left shoulder and kneeling carefully he washed his hand in the ocean and held it there, submerged, for more than a minute watching the blood trail away and the steady movement of the water against his hand as the boat moved.

"He has slowed much," he said.

The old man would have liked to keep his hand in the salt water longer but he was afraid of another sudden lurch by the fish and he stood up and braced himself and held his hand up against the sun. It was only a line burn that had cut his flesh. But it was in the working part of his hand. He knew he would need his hands before this was over and he did not like to be cut before it started.

He knelt down and found the tuna under the stern with the gaff and drew it toward him keeping it clear of the coiled lines. Holding the line with his left shoulder again, and bracing on his left hand and arm, he took the tuna off the gaff hook and put the gaff back in place. He put one knee on the fish and cut strips of dark red meat longitudinally from the back of the head to the tail. They were wedge-shaped strips and he cut them from next to the back bone down to the edge of the belly. When he had cut six strips he spread them out on the wood of the bow, wiped his knife on his trousers, and lifted the carcass of the bonito by the tail and dropped it overboard.

"I don't think I can eat an entire one," he said and drew his knife across one of the strips. He could feel the steady hard pull of the line and his left hand was cramped. It drew up tight on the heavy cord and he looked at it in disgust.

"What kind of a hand is that," he said. "Cramp then if you

want. Make yourself into a claw. It will do you no good."

Come on, he thought and looked down into the dark water at the slant of the line. Eat it now and it will strengthen the hand. It is not the hand's fault and you have been many hours with the fish. But you can stay with him for ever. Eat the bonito now.

He picked up a piece and put it in his mouth and chewed it slowly. It was not unpleasant.

Chew it well, he thought, and get all the juices. It would not be bad to eat with a little lime or with lemon or with salt.

"How do you feel, hand?" he asked the cramped hand that was almost as stiff as rigor mortis. "I'll eat some more for you."

He ate the other part of the piece that he had cut in two. He chewed it carefully and then spat out the skin.

"How does it go, hand? Or is it too early to know?"

He took another full piece and chewed it.

"It is a strong full-blooded fish," he thought. "I was lucky to get him instead of dolphin. Dolphin is too sweet. This is hardly sweet at all and all the strength is still in it."

Slowly and conscientiously he ate all of the wedge-shaped strips of fish.

He straightened up, wiping his hand on his trousers.

"Now", he said. "You can let the cord go, hand, and I will handle him with the right arm alone until you stop that nonsense." He put his left foot on the heavy line that the left hand had held and lay back against the pull against his back.

"God help me to have the cramp go," he said. "Because I do not know what the fish is going to do."

But he seems calm, he thought, and following his plan. But what is his plan, he thought. And what is mine? Mine I must improvise to his because of his great size. If he will jump I can kill him. But he stays down for ever. Then I will stay down with him for ever.

He rubbed the cramped hand against his trousers and tried to gentle the fingers. But it would not open. Maybe it will open with the sun, he thought. Maybe it will open when the strong raw tuna is digested. If I have to have it, I will open it, cost whatever it costs. But I do not want to open it now by force. Let it open by itself and come back of its own accord. After all I abused it much in the night when it was necessary to free and unite the various lines.

He thought of how some men feared being out of sight of land in a small boat and knew they were right in the months of sudden bad weather. But now they were in hurricane months and, when there are no hurricanes, the weather of hurricane months is the best of all the year.

Then, with his right hand he felt the difference in the pull of the line before he saw the slant change in the water. Then, as he leaned against the line and slapped his left hand hard and fast against his thigh he saw the line slanting slowly upward.

"He's coming up," he said. "Come on hand. Please come on."

The line rose slowly and steadily and then the surface of the ocean bulged ahead of the boat and the fish came out. He came out unendingly and water poured from his sides. He was bright in the sun and his head and back were dark purple and in the sun the stripes on his sides showed wide and a light lavender. His sword was as long as a baseball bat and tapered like a rapier and he rose his full length from the water and then re-entered it, smoothly, like a diver and the old man saw the great scythe-blade of his tail go under and the line commenced to race out.

"He is two feet longer than the skiff," the old man said. The line was going out fast but steadily and the fish was not panicked. The old man was trying with both hands to keep the line just inside of breaking strength. He knew that if he could not slow the fish with a steady pressure the fish could take out all the line and break it.

He ist a great fish and I must convince him, he thought. I must never let him learn his strength nor what he could do if he made his run. If I were him I would put in everything now and go until something broke. But, thank God, they are not as intelligent as we who kill them; although they are more noble and more able.

The old man had seen many great fish. He had seen many that weighed more than a thousand pounds and he had caught two of that size in his life, but never alone. Now alone, and out of sight of land, he was fast to the biggest fish that he had ever seen and bigger than he had ever heard of, and his left hand was still as tight as the gripped claws of an eagle.

It will uncramp though, he thought. Surely it will uncramp to help my right hand. There are three things that are brothers: the fish and my two hands. It must uncramp. It is unworthy of it to be cramped. The fish had slowed again and was going at his usual pace.

I wonder why he jumped, the old man thought. He jumped almost as though to show me how big he was. I know now, anyway, he thought. I wish I could show him what sort of man I am. But then he would see the cramped hand. Let him think I am more man than I am and I will be so. I wish I was the fish, he thought, with everything he has against only my will and my intelligence.

He settled comfortably against the wood and took his suffering as it came and the fish swam steadily and the boat moved slowly through the dark water. There was a small sea rising with the wind coming up from the east and at noon the old man's left hand was uncramped.

"Bad news for you, fish," he said and shifted the line over the sacks that covered his shoulders.

The sun was hot now although the breeze was rising gently.

"I had better rebait that little line out over the stern," he said. "If the fish decides to stay another night I will need to eat again and the water is low in the bottle. I don't think I can get anything but a dolphin here. But if I eat him fresh enough he won't be bad. I wish a flying fish would come on board tonight. But I have no light to attract them. A flying fish is excellent to eat raw and I would not have to cut him up. I must save all my strength now. Christ, I did not know he was so big."

"I'll kill him though," he said. "In all his greatness and his glory."

Although it is unjust, he thought. But I will show him what a man can do and what a man endures.

"I told the boy I was a strange old man," he said. "Now is when I must prove it."

The thousand times that he had proved it meant nothing. Now he was proving it again. Each time was a new time and he never thought about the past when he was doing it.

I wish he'd sleep and I could sleep and dream about the lions, he thought. Why are the lions the main thing that is left? Don't think, old man, he said to himself. Rest gently now against the wood and think of nothing. He is working. Work as little as you can.

It was getting into the afternoon and the boat still moved slowly and steadily. But there was an added drag now from the easterly breeze and the old man rode gently with the small sea and the hurt of the cord across his back came to him easily and smoothly.

Once in the afternoon the line started to rise again. But the fish only continued to swim at a slightly higher level. The sun was on the old man's left arm and shoulder and on his back. So he knew the fish had turned east of north.

Now that he had seen him once, he could picture the fish swimming in the water with his purple pectoral fins set wide as wings and the great erect tail slicing through the dark I wonder how much he sees at that depth, the old man thought. His eye is huge and a horse, with much less eye, can see in the dark. Once I could see quite well in the dark. Not in the absolute dark. But almost as a cat sees.

The sun and his steady movement of his fingers had uncramped his left hand now completely and he began to shift more of the strain to it and he shrugged the muscles of his back to shift the hurt of the cord a little.

"If you're not tired, fish," he said aloud, "you must be very strange."

Just before it was dark, as they passed a great island of

Sargasso weed that heaved and swung in the light sea his small line was taken by a dolphin. He saw it first when it jumped in the air, true gold in the last of the sun and bending and flapping wildly in the air. It jumped again and again in the acrobatics of its fear and he worked his way back to the stern and crouching and holding the big line with his right hand and arm, he pulled the dolphin in with his left hand, stepping on the gained line each time with his bare left foot. When the fish was at the stern, plunging and cutting from side to side in desperation, the old man leaned over the stern and lifted the burnished gold fish with its purple spots over the stern. Its jaws were working convulsively in quick bites against the hook and it pounded the bottom of the skiff with its long flat body, its tail and its head until he clubbed it across the shining golden head until it shivered and was still.

The old man unhooked the fish, rebaited the line with another sardine and tossed it over. Then he worked his way slowly back to the bow. He washed his left hand and wiped it on his trousers. Then he shifted the heavy line from his right hand to his left and washed his right hand in the sea while he watched the sun go into the ocean and the slant of the big cord.

"He hasn't changed at all," he said. But watching the movement of the water against his hand he noted that it was perceptibly slower.

"I'll lash the two oars together across the stern and that will slow him in the night," he said. "He's good for the night and so am I."

It would be better to gut the dolphin a little later to save the blood in the meat, he thought. I can do that a little later and lash the oars to make a drag at the same time. I had better keep the fish quiet now and not disturb him too much at sunset. The setting of the sun is a difficult time for all fish.

He let his hand dry in the air, then grasped the line with it and eased himself as much as he could and allowed himself to be pulled forward against the wood so that the boat took the strain as much, or more, than he did.

I'm learning how to do it, he thought. This part of it anyway. Then too, remember he hasn't eaten since he took the bait and he is huge and needs much food. I have eaten the whole bonito. Tomorrow I will eat the dolphin. He called it *dorado*. Perhaps I should eat some of it when I clean it. It will be harder to eat than the bonito. But, then, nothing is easy.

"How do you feel, fish?" he asked aloud. "I feel good and my left hand is better and I have food for a night and a day. Pull the boat, fish."

He did not truly feel good because the pain from the cord across his back had almost passed pain and gone into a dullness that he mistrusted. But I have had worse things than that, he thought. My hand is only cut a little and the cramp is gone from the other. My legs are all right. Also now I have gained on him in the question of sustenance.

It was dark now as it becomes dark quickly after the sun sets in September. He lay against the worn wood of the bow and rested all that he could. The first stars were out. He did not know the name of Rigel but he saw it and knew soon they would all be out and he would have all his distant friends.

"The fish is my friend too," he said aloud. "I have never seen or heard of such a fish. But I must kill him. I am glad we do not have to try to kill the stars."

Imagine if each day a man must try to kill the moon, he thought. The moon runs away. But imagine if a man each day should have to try to kill the sun? We were born lucky, he thought.

Then he was sorry for the great fish that had nothing to eat and his determination to kill him never relaxed in his sorrow for him. How many people will he feed, he thought. But are they worthy to eat him? No, of course not. There is no one worthy of eating him from the manner of his behaviour and his great dignity.

I do not understand these things, he thought. But it is good that we do not have to try to kill the sun or the moon or the stars. It is enough to live on the sea and kill our true brothers.

Now, he thought, I must think about the drag. It has its perils and its merits. I may lose so much line that I will lose him, if he makes his effort and the drag made by the oars is in place and the boat loses all her lightness. Her lightness prolongs both our suffering but it is my safety since he has great speed that he has never yet employed. No matter what passes I must gut the dolphin so he does not spoil and eat some of him to be strong.

Now I will rest an hour more and feel that he is solid and steady before I move back to the stern to do the work and make the decision. In the meantime I can see how he acts and if he shows any changes. The oars are a good trick; but it has reached the time to play for safety! He is much fish still and I saw that the hook was in the corner of his mouth and he has kept his mouth tight shut. The punishment of the hook is nothing. The punishment of hunger, and that he is against something that he does not comprehend, is everything. Rest now, old man, and let him work until your next duty comes.

He rested for what he believed to be two hours. The moon did not rise now until late and he had no way of judging the time. Nor was he really resting except comparatively. He was still bearing the pull of the fish across his shoulders but he placed his left hand on the gunwale of the bow and confided more and more of the resistance to the fish to the skiff itself.

How simple it would be if I could make the line fast, he thought. But with one small lurch he could break it. I must cushion the pull of the line with my body and at all times be ready to give line with both hands.

"But you have not slept yet, old man," he said aloud. "It is half a day and a night and now another day and you have not slept. You must devise a way so that you sleep a little if he is quiet and steady. If you do not sleep you might become unclear in the head."

He held the line tight in his right hand and then pushed his thigh against his right hand as he leaned all his weight against the wood of the bow. Then he passed the line a little lower on his shoulders and braced his left hand on it.

My right hand can hold it as long as it is braced, he thought. If it relaxes in sleep my left hand will wake me as the line goes out. It is hard on the right hand. But he is used to punishment. Even if I sleep twenty minutes or a half an hour it is good.

He lay forward cramping himself against the line with all of his body, putting all his weight on to his right hand, and he was asleep.

He dreamed that he was in the village on his bed and there was a norther and he was very cold and his right arm was asleep because his head had rested on it instead of a pillow.

After that he began to dream of the long yellow beach and he saw the first of the lions come down onto it in the early dark and then the other lions came and he rested his chin on the wood of the bows where the ship lay anchored with the evening off-shore breeze and he waited to see if there would be more lions and he was happy.

The moon had been up for a long time but he slept on and the fish pulled on steadily and the boat moved into the tunnel of clouds.

He woke with the jerk of his right fist coming up against his face and the line burning out through his right hand. He had no feeling of his left hand but he braked all he could with his right and the line rushed out. Finally his left hand found the line and he leaned back against the line and now it burned his back and his left hand, and his left hand was taking all the strain and cutting badly. He looked back at the coils of line and they were feeding smoothly. Just then the fish jumped making a great bursting of the ocean and then a heavy fall. Then he jumped again and again and the boat was going fast although line was still racing out and the old man was raising the strain to breaking point and raising it to breaking point again and again. He had been pulled down tight on to the bow and his face was in the cut slice of dolphin and he could not move.

This is what we waited for, he thought. So now let us take it.

Make him pay for the line, he thought. Make him pay for it.

He could not see the fish's jumps but only heard the breaking of the ocean and the heavy splash as he fell. The speed of the line was cutting his hands badly but he had always known this would happen and he tried to keep the cutting across the calloused parts and not let the line slip into the palm or cut the fingers.

If the boy was here he would wet the coils of line, he thought. Yes. If the boy were here. If the boy were here.

The old man held him with his left hand and his shoulders now and stooped down and scooped up water in his right hand to get the crushed dolphin flesh off of his face. He was afraid that it might nauseate him and he would vomit and lose his strength. When his face was cleaned he washed his right hand in the water over the side and then let it stay in the salt water while he watched the first light come before the sunrise. He's headed almost east, he thought. That means he is tired and going with the current. Soon he will have to circle. Then our true work begins.

After he judged that his right hand had been in the water long enough he took it out and looked at it.

"It is not bad," he said. "And pain does not matter to a man."

The sun was rising for the third time since he had put to sea when the fish started to circle.

He could not see by the slant of the line that the fish was circling. It was too early for that. He just felt a faint slackening of the pressure of the line and he commenced to pull on it gently with his right hand. It tightened, as always, but just when he reached the point where it would break, line began to come in. He slipped his shoulders and head from under the line and began to pull in line steadily and gently. He used both of his hands in a swinging motion and tried to do the pulling as much as he could with his body and his legs. His old legs and shoulders pivoted with the swinging of the pulling.

"It is a very big circle," he said. "But he is circling."

Then the line would not come in any more and he held it until he saw the drops jumping from it in the sun. Then it started out and the old man knelt down and let it go grudgingly back into the dark water.

"He is making the far part of his circle now," he said. I must hold all I can, he thought. The strain will shorten his circle each time. Perhaps in an hour I will see him. Now I must convince him and then I must kill him.

But the fish kept on circling slowly and the old man was wet with sweat and tired deep into his bones two hours later. But the circles were much shorter now and from the way the line slanted he could tell the fish had risen steadily while he swam.

For an hour the old man had been seeing black spots before his eyes and the sweat salted his eyes and salted the cut over his eye and on his forehand. He was not afraid of the black spots. They were normal at the tension that he was pulling on the line. Twice, though, he had felt faint and dizzy and that had worried him.

"I could not fail myself and die on a fish like this," he said. "Now that I have him coming so beautifully, God help me endure. I'll say a hundred Our Fathers and a hundred Hail Marys. But I cannot say them now."

Consider them said, he thought. I'll say them later.

Just then he felt a sudden banging and jerking on the line he held with his two hands. It was sharp and hard-feeling and heavy.

He is hitting the wire leader with his spear, he thought. That was bound to come. He had to do that. It may make him jump though and I would rather he stayed circling now. The jumps were necessary for him to take air. But after that each one can widen the opening of the hook wound and he can throw the hook.

"Don't jump, fish," he said. "Don't jump."

The fish hit the wire several times more and each time he shook his head the old man gave up a little line.

I must hold his pain where it is, he thought. Mine does not

matter. I can control mine. But his pain could drive him mad.

After a while the fish stopped beating at the wire and started circling slowly again. The old man was gaining line steadily now. But he felt faint again. He lifted some sea water with his left hand and put it on his head. Then he put more on and rubbed the back of his neck.

"I have no cramps," he said. "He'll be up soon and I can last. You have to last. Don't even speak of it."

He kneeled against the bow and, for a moment, slipped the line over his back again. I'll rest now while he goes out on the circle and then stand up and work on him when he comes in, he decided.

It was a great temptation to rest in the bow and let the fish make one circle by himself without recovering any line. But when the strain showed the fish had turned to come toward the boat, the old man rose to his feet and started the pivoting and the weaving pulling that brought in all the line he gained.

I'm tireder than I have ever been, he thought, and now the trade wind is rising. But that will be good to take him in with. I need that badly.

"I'll rest on the next turn as he goes out," he said. "I feel much better. Then in two or three turns more I will have him."

His straw hat was far on the back of his head and he sank down into the bow with the pull of the line as he felt the fish turn.

You work now, fish, he thought. I'll take you at the turn.

The sea had risen considerably. But it was a fair-weather breeze and he had to have it to get home.

"I'll just steer south and west," he said. "A man is never lost at sea and it is a long island."

It was on the third turn that he saw the fish first.

He saw him first as a dark shadow that took so long to pass under the boat that he could not believe its length.

"No," he said. "He can't be that big."

But he was that big and at the end of this circle he came to the surface only thirty yards away and the man saw his tail out of water. It was higher than a big scythe blade and a very pale lavender above the dark blue water. It raked back and as the fish swam just below the surface the old man could see his huge bulk and the purple stripes that banded him. His dorsal fin was down and his huge pectorals were spread wide.

On this circle the old man could see the fish's eye and the two grey sucking fish that swam around him. Sometimes they attached themselves to him. Sometimes they darted off. Sometimes they would swim easily in his shadow. They were each over three feet long and when they swam fast they lashed their whole bodies like eels.

The old man was sweating now but from something else besides the sun. On each calm placid turn the fish made he was gaining line and he was sure that in two turns more he would have a chance to get the harpoon in.

But I must get him close, close, close, he thought. I mustn't try for the head. I must get the heart.

"Be calm and strong, old man," he said.

On the next circle the fish's back was out but he was a little too far from the boat. On the next circle he was still too far away but he was higher out of water and the old man was sure that by gaining some more line he could have him alongside.

He had rigged his harpoon long before and its coil of light rope was in a round basket and the end was made fast to the bitt in the bow.

The fish was coming in on his circle now calm and beautiful-looking and only his great tail moving. The old man pulled on him all that he could to bring him closer. For just a moment the fish turned a little on his side. Then he straightened himself and began another circle.

"I moved him," the old man said. "I moved him then."

He felt faint again now but he held on the great fish all the strain that he could. I moved him, he thought. Maybe this time I can get him over. Pull, hands, he thought. Hold up, legs. Last for me, head. Last for me. You never went. This time I'll pull him over.

But when he put all of his effort on, starting it well out before the fish came alongside and pulling with all his strength, the fish pulled part way over and then righted himself and swam away.

"Fish," the old man said. "Fish, you are going to have to die anyway. Do you have to kill me too?"

That way nothing is accomplished, he thought. His mouth was too dry to speak but he could not reach for the water now. I must get him alongside this time, he thought. I am not good for many more turns. Yes you are, he told himself. You're good for ever.

On the next turn, he nearly had him. But again the fish righted himself and swam slowly away.

You are killing me, fish, the old man thought. But you have a right to. Never have I seen a greater, or more beautiful, or a calmer or more noble thing than you, brother. Come on and kill me. I do not care who kills who.

Now you are getting confused in the head, he thought. You must keep your head clear. Keep your head clear and know how to suffer like a man. Or a fish, he thought.

"Clear up, head," he said in a voice he could hardly hear. "Clear up."

Twice more it was the same on the turns.

I do not know, the old man thought. He had been on the point of feeling himself go each time. I do not know. But I will try it once more.

He tried it once more and he felt himself going when he turned the fish. The fish righted himself and swam off again slowly with the great tail weaving in the air.

I'll try it again, the old man promised, although his hands were mushy now and he could only see well in flashes.

He tried it again and it was the same. So, he thought, and he felt himself going before he started; I will try it once again.

He took all his pain and what was left of his strength and his long gone pride and he put it against the fish's agony and the fish came over on to his side and swam gently on his side, his bill almost touching the planking of the skiff, and started to pass the boat, long, deep, wide, silver and barred with purple and interminable in the water.

The old man dropped the line and put his foot on it and lifted the harpoon as high as he could and drove it down with all his strength, and more strength he had just summoned, into the fish's side just behind the great chest fin that rose high in the air to the altitude of the man's chest. He felt the iron go in and he leaned on it and drove it further and then pushed all his weight after it.

Then the fish came alive, with his death in him, and rose high out of the water showing all his great length and width and all his power and his beauty. He seemed to hang in the air above the old man in the skiff. Then he fell into the water with a crash that sent spray over the old man and over all of the skiff.

The old man felt faint and sick and he could not see well. But he cleared the harpoon line and let it run slowly through his raw hands and, when he could see, he saw the fish was on his back with his silver belly up. The shaft of the harpoon was projecting at an angle from the fish's shoulder and the sea was discolouring with the red of the blood from his heart. First it was dark as a shoal in the blue water that was more than a mile deep. Then it spread like a cloud. The fish was silvery and still and floated with the waves.

The old man looked carefully in the glimpse of vision that he had. Then he took two turns of the harpoon line around the bitt in the bow and laid his head on his hands.

"Keep my head clear," he said against the wood of the bow. "I am a tired old man. But I have killed this fish which is my brother and now I must do the slave work."

Now I must prepare the nooses and the rope to lash him alongside, he thought. Even if we were two and swamped her to load him and bailed her out, this skiff would never hold him.

I must prepare everything, then bring him in and lash him well and step the mast and set sail for home.

He started to pull the fish in to have him alongside so that he could pass a line through his gills and out his mouth and make his head fast alongside the bow. I want to see him, he thought, and to touch and to feel him. He is my fortune, he thought. But that is not why I wish to feel him. I think I felt his heart, he thought. When I pushed on the harpoon shaft the second time. Bring him in now and make him fast and get the noose around his tail and another around his middle to bind him to the skiff.

"Get to work, old man," he said. He took a very small drink of the water. "There is very much slave work to be done now that the fight is over."

He looked up at the sky and then out to his fish. He looked at the sun carefully. It is not much more than noon, he thought. And the trade wind is rising. The lines all mean nothing now. The boy and I will splice them when we are home.

"Come on, fish," he said. But the fish did not come. Instead he lay there wallowing now in the seas and the old man pulled the skiff up on to him.

When he was even with him and had the fish's head against the bow he could not believe his size. But he untied the harpoon rope from the bitt, passed it through the fish's gills and out his jaws, made a turn around his sword, then passed the rope through the other gill, made another turn around the bill and knotted the double rope and made it fast to the bitt in the bow. He cut the rope then and went astern to noose the tail. The fish had turned silver from his original purple and silver, and the stripes showed the same pale violet colour as his tail. They were wider than a man's hand with his fingers spread and the fish's eye looked as detached as the mirrors in a periscope or as a saint in a procession.

"It was the only way to kill him," the old man said. He was feeling better since the water and he knew he would not go away and his head was clear. He's over fifteen hundred pounds the way he is, he thought. Maybe much more. If he dresses out two-thirds of that at thirty cents a pound?

"I need a pencil for that," he said. "My head is not that clear. But I think the great DiMaggio would be proud of me today."

He made the fish fast to bow and stern and to the middle thwart. He was so big it was like lashing a much bigger skiff alongside. He cut a piece of line and tied the fish's lower jaw against his bill so his mouth would not open and they would sail as cleanly as possible. Then he stepped the mast and, with the stick that was his gaff and with his boom rigged, the patched sail drew, the boat began to move, and half lying in the stern he sailed south-west.

He did not need a compass to tell him where south-west was. He only needed the feel of the trade wind and the drawing of the sail. I better put a small line out with a spoon on it and try and get something to eat and drink for the moisture. But he could not find a spoon and his sardines were rotten. So he hooked a patch of yellow Gulf weed with the gaff as they passed and shook it so that the small shrimps that were in it fell on to the planking of the skiff. There were more than a dozen of them and they jumped and kicked like sand fleas. The old man pinched their heads off with his thumb and forefinger and ate them chewing up the shells and the tails. They were very tiny but he knew they were nourishing and they tasted good.

Now he knew there was the fish and his hands and back were no dream. The hands cure quickly, he thought. I bled them clean and the salt water will heal them. The dark water of the true gulf is the greatest healer that there is. All I must do is keep the head clear. The hands have done their work and we sail well. With his mouth shut and his tail straight up and down we sail like brothers. Then his head started to become a little unclear and he thought, is he bringing me in or am I bringing him in? If I were towing him behind there would be no question. Nor if the fish were in the skiff, with all dignity gone, there would be no question either. But they were sailing together lashed side by side and the old man thought, let him bring me in if it pleases him. I am only better than him through trickery and he meant me no harm.

They sailed well and the old man soaked his hands in the salt water and tried to keep his head clear. There were high cumulus clouds and enough cirrus above them so that the old man knew the breeze would last all night. The old man looked at the fish constantly to make sure it was true. It was an hour before the first shark hit him.

The shark was not an accident. He had come up from deep down in the water as the dark cloud of blood had settled and dispersed in the mile-deep sea. He had come up so fast and absolutely without caution that he broke the surface of the blue water and was in the sun. Then he fell back into the sea and picked up the scent and started swimming on the course the skiff and the fish had taken.

Sometimes he lost the scent. But he would pick it up again, or have just a trace of it, and he swam fast and hard on the course. He was a very big Mako shark built to swim as fast as the fastest fish in the sea and everything about him was beautiful except his jaws. His back was as blue as a swordfish's and his belly was silver and his hide was smooth and handsome. He was built as a swordfish except for his huge jaws which were tight shut now as he swam fast, just under the surface with his high dorsal fin knifing through the water without wavering. Inside the closed double lip of his jaws all of his eight rows of teeth were slanted inwards. They were not the ordinary pyramid-shaped teeth of most sharks. They were shaped like a man's fingers when they are crisped like claws. They were nearly as long as the fingers of the old man and they had razor-sharp cutting edges on both sides. This was a fish built to feed on all the fishes in the sea, that were so fast and strong and well armed that they had no other enemy. Now he speeded up as he smelled the fresher scent and his blue dorsal fin cut the water.

When the old man saw him coming he knew that this was a shark that had no fear at all and would do exactly what he wished. He prepared the harpoon and made the rope fast while he watched the shark come on. The rope was short as it lacked what he had cut away to lash the fish.

The old man's head was clear and good now and he was full of resolution but he had little hope. It was too good to last, he thought. He took one look at the great fish as he watched the shark close in. It might as well have been a dream, he thought. I cannot keep him from hitting me but maybe I can get him. *Dentuso*, he thought. Bad luck to your mother.

The shark closed fast astern and when he hit the fish the old man saw his mouth open and his strange eyes and the clicking chop of the teeth as he drove forward in the meat just above the tail. The shark's head was out of water and his back was coming out and the old man could hear the noise of skin and flesh ripping on the big fish when he rammed the harpoon down on to the shark's head at a spot where the line between his eyes intersected with the line that ran straight back from his nose. There were no such lines. There was only the heavy sharp blue head and the big eyes and the clicking, thrusting all-swallowing jaws. But that was the location of the brain and the old man hit it. He hit it with his blood-mushed hands driving a good harpoon with all his strength. He hit it without hope but with resolution and complete malignancy.

The shark swung over and the old man saw his eye was not alive and then he swung over once again, wrapping himself in two loops of the rope. The old man knew that he was dead but the shark would not accept it. Then, on his back, with tail lashing and his jaws clicking, the shark ploughed over the water as a speed-boat does. The water was white where his tail beat it and threequarters of his body was clear above the water when the rope came taut, shivered, and then snapped. The shark lay quietly for a little while on the surface and the old man watched him. Then he went down very slowly.

"He took about forty pounds," the old man said aloud. He took my harpoon too and all the rope, he thought, and now my fish bleeds again and there will be others.

He did not like to look at the fish any more since he had been mutilated. When the fish had been hit it was as though he himself were hit.

But I killed the shark that hit my fish, he thought. And he was the biggest *dentuso* that I have ever seen. And God knows that I have seen big ones.

It was too good to last, he thought. I wish it had been a dream now and that I had never hooked the fish and was alone in bed on the newspapers.

"But man is not made for defeat," he said. "A man can be destroyed but not defeated." I am sorry that I killed the fish though, he thought. Now the bad time is coming and I do not even have the harpoon. The *dentuso* is cruel and able and strong and intelligent. But I was more intelligent than he was. Perhaps not, he thought. Perhaps I was only better armed.

"Don't think, old man," he said aloud. "Sail on this course and take it when it comes."

He knew quite well the pattern of what could happen when he reached the inner part of the current. But there was nothing to be done now.

"Yes, there is," he said aloud. "I can lash my knife to the butt of one of the oars."

So he did that with the tiller under his arm and the sheet of the sail under his foot.

"Now," he said. "I am still an old man. But I am not unarmed."

The breeze was fresh now and he sailed on well. He watched only the forward part of the fish and some of his hope returned.

It is silly not to hope, he thought. Besides I believe it is a sin. Do not think about sin, he thought. There are enough problems now without sin. Also I have no understanding of it.

I have no understanding of it and I am not sure that I believe in it. Perhaps it was a sin to kill the fish. I suppose it was even though I did it to keep me alive and feed many people. But then everything is a sin. Do not think about sin. It is much too late for that and there are people who are paid to do it. Let them think about it. You were born to be a fisherman as the fish was born to be a fish. San Pedro was a fisherman as was the father of the great DiMaggio.

But he liked to think about all things that he was involved in and since there was nothing to read and he did not have a radio, he thought much and he kept on thinking about sin. You did not kill the fish only to keep alive and to sell for food, he thought. You killed him for pride and because you are a fisherman. You loved him when he was alive and you loved him after. If you love him, it is not a sin to kill him. Or is it more?

"You think too much, old man," he said aloud.

But you enjoyed killing the *dentuso,* he thought. He lives on the live fish as you do. He is not a scavenger nor just a moving appetite as some sharks are. He is beautiful and noble and knows no fear of anything.

"I killed him in self-defence," the old man said aloud. "And I killed him well."

Besides, he thought, everything kills everything else in some way. Fishing kills me exactly as it keeps me alive. The boy keeps me alive, he thought. I must not deceive myself too much.

He leaned over the side and pulled loose a piece of the meat of the fish where the shark had cut him. He chewed it and noted its quality and its good taste. It was firm and juicy, like meat, but it was not red. There was no stringiness in it and he knew that it would bring the highest price in the market. But there was no way to keep its scent out of the water and the old man knew that a very bad time was coming.

The breeze was steady. It had backed a little further into the north-east and he knew that meant that it would not fall off. The old man looked ahead of him but he could see no sails nor could he see the hull nor the smoke of any ship. There were only the flying fish that went up from his bow sailing away to either side and the yellow patches of Gulf weed. He could not even see a bird.

He had sailed for two hours, resting in the stern and sometimes chewing a bit of the meat from the marlin, trying to rest and to be strong, when he saw the first of the two sharks.

"*Ay*," he said aloud. There is no translation for this word and perhaps it is just a noise such as a man might make, involuntarily, feeling the nail go through his hands and into the wood.

"*Galanos*," he said aloud. He had seen the second fin now coming up behind the first and had identified them as shovel-nosed sharks by the brown, triangular fin and the sweeping movements of the tail. They had the scent and were excited and in the stupidity of their great hunger they were losing and finding the scent in their excitement. But they were closing all the time.

The old man made the sheet fast and jammed the tiller. Then he took up the oar with the knife lashed to it. He lifted it as lightly as he could because his hands rebelled at the pain. Then he opened and closed them on it lightly to loosen them. He closed them firmly so they would take the pain now and would not flinch and watched the sharks come. He could see their wide, flattened, shovel-pointed heads now and their white-tipped wide pectoral fins. They were hateful sharks, bad-smelling, scavengers as well as killers, and when they were hungry they would bite at an oar or the rudder of a boat. It was these sharks that would cut the turtles' legs and flippers off when the turtles were asleep on the surface, and they would hit a man in the water, if they were hungry, even if the man had no smell of fish blood nor of fish slime on him.

"*Ay*," the old man said. "*Galanos*. Come on, *Galanos*."

They came. But they did not come as the Mako had come. One turned and went out of sight under the skiff and the old man could feel the skiff shake as he jerked and pulled on the fish. The other watched the old man with his slitted yellow eyes and then came in fast with his half circle of jaws wide to hit the fish where he had already been bitten. The line showed clearly on the top of his brown head and back where the brain joined the spinal cord and the old man drove the knife on the oar into the juncture, withdrew it, and drove it in again into the shark's yellow cat-like eyes. The shark let go of the fish and slid down, swallowing what he had taken as he died.

The skiff was still shaking with the destruction the other shark was doing to the fish and the old man let go the sheet so that the skiff would swing broadside and bring the shark out from under. When he saw the shark he leaned over the side and punched at him. He hit only meat and the hide was set hard and he barely got the knife in. The blow hurt not only his hands but his shoulder too. But the shark came up fast with his head out and the old man hit him squarely in the centre of his flat-topped head as his nose came out of water and lay against the fish. The old man withdrew the blade and punched the shark exactly in the same spot again. He still hung to the fish with his jaws locked and the old man stabbed him in his left eye. The shark still hung there.

"No?" the old man said and he drove the blade between the vertebrae and the brain. It was an easy shot now and he felt the cartilage sever. The old man reversed the oar and put the blade between the shark's jaws to open them. He twisted the blade and as the shark slid loose he said, "Go on, *galano*. Slide down a mile deep. Go and see your friend, or maybe it's your mother."

The old man wiped the blade of his knife and laid down the oar. Then he found the sheet and the sail filled and he brought the skiff on to her course.

"They must have taken a quarter of him and of the best meat." he said aloud. "I wish it were a dream and that I had never hooked him. I'm sorry about it, fish. It makes everything wrong." He stopped and he did not want to look at the fish now. Drained of blood and awash he looked the colour of the silver backing of a mirror and his stripes still showed.

"I shouldn't have gone out so far, fish," he said. "Neither for you nor for me. I'm sorry, fish."

Now, he said to himself. Look to the lashing on the knife and see if it has been cut. Then get your hand in order because there still is more to come.

"I wish I had a stone for the knife," the old man said after he had checked the lashing on the oar butt. "I should have brought a stone." You should have brought many things, he thought. But you did not bring them, old man. Now is no time to think of what you do not have. Think of what you can do with what there is.

"You give me much good counsel," he said aloud. "I'm tired of it."

He held the tiller under his arm and soaked both his hands in the water as the skiff drove forward.

"God knows how much that last one took," he said. "But she's much lighter now." He did not want to think of the mutilated under-side of the fish. He knew that each of the jerking bumps of the shark had been meat torn away and that the fish now made a trail for all sharks as wide as a highway through the sea.

He was a fish to keep a man all winter, he thought. Don't think of that. Just rest and try to get your hands in shape to defend what is left of him. The blood smell from my hands means nothing now with all that scent in the water. Besides they do not bleed much. There is nothing cut that means anything. The bleeding may keep the left from cramping.

What can I think of now? he thought. Nothing. I must think of nothing and wait for the next ones. I wish it had really been a dream, he thought. But who knows? It might have turned out well.

The next shark that came was a single shovelnose. He came like a pig to the trough if a pig had a mouth so wide that you could put your head in it. The old man let him hit the fish and then drove the knife on the oar down into his brain. But the shark jerked backwards as he rolled and the knife blade snapped.

The old man settled himself to steer. He did not even watch the big shark sinking slowly in the water, showing first life-size, then small, then tiny. That always fascinated the old man. But he did not even watch it now.

"I have the gaff now," he said. "But it will do no good. I have the two oars and the tiller and the short club."

Now they have beaten me, he thought. I am too old to club sharks to death. But I will try it as long as I have the oars and the short club and the tiller.

He put his hands in the water again to soak them. It was getting late in the afternoon and he saw nothing but the sea and the sky. There was more wind in the sky than there had been, and soon he hoped that he would see land.

"You're tired, old man," he said. "You're tired inside."

The sharks did not hit him again until just before sunset.

The old man saw the brown fins coming along the wide trail the fish must make in the water. They were not even quartering on the scent. They were headed straight for the skiff swimming side by side.

He jammed the tiller, made the sheet fast and reached under the stern for the club. It was an oar handle from a broken oar sawed off to about two and a half feet in length. He could only use it effectively with one hand because of the grip of the handle and he took good hold of it with his right hand, flexing his hand on it, as he watched the sharks come. They were both *galanos*.

I must let the first one get a good hold and hit him on the point of the nose or straight across the top of the head, he thought.

The two sharks closed together and as he saw the one nearest him open his jaws and sink them into the silver side of the fish, he raised the club high and brought it down heavy and slamming on to the top of the shark's broad head. He felt the rubbery solidity as the club came down. But he felt the rigidity of bone too and he struck the shark once more hard across the point of the nose as he slid down from the fish.

The other shark had been in and out and now came in again with his jaws wide. The old man could see pieces of the meat of the fish spilling white from the corner of his jaws as he bumped the fish and closed his jaws. He swung at him and hit only the head and the shark looked at him and wrenched the meat loose. The old man swung the club down on him again as he slipped away to swallow and hit only the heavy solid rubberyness.

"Come on, *galano,*" the old man said. "Come in again."

The shark came in in a rush and the old man hit him as he shut his jaws. He hit him solidly and from as high up as he could raise the club. This time he felt the bone at the base of the brain and he hit him again in the same place while the shark tore the meat loose sluggishly and slid down from the fish.

The old man watched for him to come again but neither shark showed. Then he saw one on the surface swimming in circles. He did not see the fin of the other.

I could not expect to kill them, he thought. I could have in my time. But I have hurt them both badly and neither one can feel very good. If I could have used a bat with two hands I could have killed the first one surely. Even now, he thought.

He did not want to look at the fish. He knew that half of him had been destroyed. The sun had gone down while he had been in the fight with the sharks.

"It will be dark soon," he said. "Then I should see the glow of Havana. If I am too far to the eastward I will see the light of one of the new beaches."

I cannot be too far out now, he thought. I hope no one has been too worried. There is only the boy to worry, of course. But I am sure he would have confidence. Many of the older fishermen will worry. Many others too, he thought. I live in a good town.

He could not talk to the fish any more because the fish had been ruined too badly. Then something came into his head.

"Half-fish," he said. "Fish that you were. I am sorry that I went too far out. I ruined us both. But we have killed many sharks, you and I, and ruined many others. How many did you ever kill, old fish? You do not have that spear on your head for nothing."

He liked to think of the fish and what he could do to a shark if he were swimming free. I should have chopped the bill off to fight them with, he thought. But there was no hatchet and then there was no knife.

But if I had, and could have lashed it to an oar butt, what a weapon. Then we might have fought them together. What will you do now if they come in the night? What can you do?

"Fight them," he said. "I'll fight them until I die."

But in the dark now and no glow showing and no lights and only the wind and the steady pull of the sail he felt that perhaps he was already dead. He put his two hands together and felt the palms. They were not dead and he could bring the pain of life by simply opening and closing them. He leaned his back against the stern and knew he was not dead. His shoulders told him.

I have all those prayers I promised if I caught the fish, he thought. But I am too tired to say them now. I better get the sack and put it over my shoulders.

He lay in the stern and steered and watched for the glow to come in the sky. I have half of him, he thought. Maybe I'll have the luck to bring the forward half in. I should have some luck. No, he said. You violated your luck when you went too far outside.

"Don't be silly," he said aloud. "And keep awake and steer. You may have much luck yet."

"I'd like to buy some if there's any place they sell it," he said.

What could I buy it with? he asked himself. Could I buy it with a lost harpoon and a broken knife and two bad hands?

"You might," he said. "You tried to buy it with eighty-four days at sea. They nearly sold it to you too."

I must not think nonsense, he thought. Luck is a thing that comes in many forms and who can recognize her? I would take some though in any form and pay what they asked. I wish I could see the glow from the lights, he thought. I wish too many things. But that is the thing I wish for now. He tried to settle more comfortably to steer and from his pain he knew he was not dead.

He saw the reflected glare of the lights of the city at what must have been around ten o'clock at night. They were only perceptible at first as the light is in the sky before the moon rises. Then they were steady to see across the ocean which was rough now with the increasing breeze. He steered inside of the glow and he thought that now, soon, he must hit the edge of the stream.

Now it is over, he thought. They will probably hit me again. But what can a man do against them in the dark without a weapon?

He was stiff and sore now and his wounds and all of the strained parts of his body hurt with the cold of the night. I hope I do not have to fight again, he thought. I hope so much I do not have to fight again.

But by midnight he fought and this time he knew the fight was useless. They came in a pack and he could only see the lines in the water that their fins made and their phosphorescence as they threw themselves on the fish. He clubbed at heads and heard the jaws chop and the shaking of the skiff as they took hold below. He clubbed desperately at what he could only feel and hear and he felt something seize the club and it was gone.

He jerked the tiller free from the rudder and beat and chopped with it, holding it in both hands and driving it down again and again. But they were up to the bow now and driving in one after the other and together, tearing off the pieces of meat that showed glowing below the sea as they turned to come once more.

One came, finally, against the head itself and he knew that it was over. He swung the tiller across the shark's head where the jaws were caught in the heaviness of the fish's head which would not tear. He swung it once and twice and again. He heard the tiller break and he lunged at the shark with the splintered butt. He felt it go in and knowing it was sharp he drove it in again. The shark let go and rolled away. That was the last shark of the pack that came. There was nothing more for them to eat.

The old man could hardly breathe now and he felt a strange taste in his mouth. It was coppery and sweet and he was afraid of it for a moment. But there was not much of it.

He spat into the ocean and said, "Eat that, *Galanos*. And make a dream you've killed a man."

He knew he was beaten now finally and without remedy and he went back to the stern and found the jagged end of the tiller would fit in the slot of the rudder well enough for him to steer. He settled the sack around his shoulders and put the skiff on her course. He sailed lightly now and he had no thoughts nor any feelings of any kind. He was past everything now and he sailed the skiff to make his home port as well and as intelligently as he could. In the night sharks hit the carcass as someone might pick up crumbs from the table. The old man paid no attention to them and did not pay any attention to anything except steering. He only noticed how lightly and how well the skiff sailed now there was no great weight beside her.

She's good, he thought. She is sound and not harmed in any way except for the tiller. That is easily replaced.

He could feel he was inside the current now and he could see the lights of the beach colonies along the shore. He knew where he was now and it was nothing to get home.

The wind is our friend, anyway, he thought. Then he added, sometimes. And the great sea with our friends and our enemies. And bed, he thought. Bed is my friend. Just bed, he thought. Bed will be a great thing. It is easy when you are beaten, he thought. I never knew how easy it was. And what beat you, he thought.

"Nothing," he said aloud. "I went out too far."

When he sailed into the little harbour the lights of the Terrace were out and he knew everyone was in bed. The breeze had risen steadily and was blowing strongly now. It was quiet in the harbour though and he sailed up on to the little patch of shingle below the rocks. There was no one to help him so he pulled the boat up as far as he could. Then he stepped out and made her fast to a rock.

He unstepped the mast and furled the sail and tied it. Then he shouldered the mast and started to climb. It was then he knew the depth of his tiredness. He stopped for a moment and looked back and saw in the reflection from the street light the great tail of the fish standing up well behind the skiff's stern. He saw the white naked line of his backbone and the dark mass of the head with the projecting bill and all the nakedness between.

He started to climb again and at the top he fell and lay for some time with the mast across his shoulder. He tried to get up. But it was too difficult and he sat there with the mast on his shoulder and looked at the road. A cat passed on the far side going about its business and the old man watched it. Then he just watched the road.

Finally he put the mast down and stood up. He picked the mast up and put it on his shoulder and started up the road. He had to sit down five times before he reached his shack.

Inside the shack he leaned the mast against the wall. In the dark he found a water bottle and took a drink. Then he lay down on the bed. He pulled the blanket over his shoulders and then over his back and legs and he slept face down on the newspapers with his arms out straight and the palms of his hands up.

He was asleep when the boy looked in the door in the morning. It was blowing so hard that the drifting boats would not be going out and the boy had slept late and then come to the old man's shack as he had come each morning. The boy saw that the old man was breathing and then he saw the old man's hands and he started to cry. He went out very quietly to go to bring some coffee and all the way down the road he was crying.

Many fishermen were around the skiff looking at what was lashed beside it and one was in the water, his trousers rolled up, measuring the skeleton with a length of line.

The boy did not go down. He had been there before and one of the fishermen was looking after the skiff for him.

"How is he?" one of the fishermen shouted.

"Sleeping," the boy called. He did not care that they saw him crying. "Let no one disturb him."

"He was eighteen feet from nose to tail," the fisherman who was measuring him called.

"I believe it," the boy said.

He went into the Terrace and asked for a can of coffee.

"Hot and with plenty of milk and sugar in it."

"Anything more?"

"No. Afterwards I will see what he can eat."

"What a fish it was," the proprietor said. "There has never been such a fish. Those were two fine fish you took yesterday too."

"Damn my fish," the boy said and he started to cry again.

"Do you want a drink of any kind?" the proprietor asked.

"No," the boy said. "Tell them not to bother Santiago. I'll be back."

"Tell him how sorry I am."

"Thanks," the boy said.

The boy carried the hot can of coffee up to the old man's shack and sat by him until he woke. Once it looked as though he were waking. But he had gone back into heavy sleep and the boy had gone across the road to borrow some wood to heat the coffee.

Finally the old man woke.

"Don't sit up," the boy said. "Drink this." He poured some of the coffee in a glass.

The old man took it and drank it.

"They beat me, Manolin," he said. "They truly beat me."

"*He* didn't beat you. Not the fish."

"No. Truly. It was afterwards."

"Pedrico is looking after the skiff and the gear. What do you want done with the head?"

"Let Pedrico chop it up to use in fish traps."

"And the spear?"

"You keep it if you want it."

"I want it," the boy said. "Now we must make our plans about the other things."

Did they search for me?"

"Of course. With coast guard and with planes."

"The ocean is very big and a skiff is small and hard to see," the old man said. He noticed how pleasant it was to have someone to talk to instead of speaking only to himself and to the sea. "I missed you," he said. "What did you catch?"

"One the first day. One the second and two the third."

"Very good."

"Now we fish together again."

"No. I am not lucky. I am not lucky any more."

"The hell with lucky," the boy said. "I'll bring the luck with me."

"What will your family say?"

"I do not care. I caught two yesterday. But we will fish together now for I still have much to learn."

"We must get a good killing lance and always have it on board. You can make the blade from a spring leaf from an old Ford. We can grind it in Guanabacoa. It should be sharp and not tempered so it will break. My knife broke."

"I'll get another knife and have the spring ground. How many days of heavy *brisa* have we?"

"Maybe three. Maybe more."

"I will have everything in order," the boy said. "You get your hands well, old man."

"I know how to care for them. In the night I spat something strange and felt something in my chest was broken."

"Get that well too," the boy said. "Lie down, old man, and I will bring you your clean shirt. And something to eat."

"Bring any of the papers of the time that I was gone," the old man said.

"You must get well fast for there is much that I can learn and you can teach me everything. How much did you suffer?"

"Plenty," the old man said.

"I'll bring the food and the papers," the boy said. "Rest well, old man. I will bring stuff from the drug-store for your hands."

"Don't forget to tell Pedrico the head is his."

"No. I will remember."

As the boy went out the door and down the worn coral rock road he was crying again.

That afternoon there was a party of tourists at the Terrace and looking down in the water among the empty beer cans and dead barracudas a woman saw a great long white spine with a huge tail at the end that lifted and swung with the tide while the east wind blew a heavy steady sea outside the entrance to the harbour.

"What's that?" she asked a waiter and pointed to the long backbone of the great fish that was now just garbage waiting to go out with the tide.

"Tiburon," the waiter said, "Eshark." He was meaning to explain what had happened.

"I didn't know sharks had such handsome, beautifully formed tails."

"I didn't either," her male companion said.

Up the road, in his shack, the old man was sleeping again. He was still sleeping on his face and the boy was sitting by him watching him. The old man was dreaming about the lions.

EXPLANATORY NOTES

[1] **skiff** [skif]: kleines Ruderboot; Skiff – [6] **at their orders:** auf ihr 5
Geheiß – [9] **to coil** [kɔil]: aufwickeln; aufrollen; aufschießen – [10] **gaff** [gæf]: Fischhaken; Gaffel – [10] **harpoon** [hɑːˈpuːn]: Harpune – [10] **to furl** [fəːl]: (*e.g.*, to furl a sail, flag, or umbrella) aufrollen; zusammenrollen – [11] **mast** [mɑːst]: (Schiffs-)Mast – [13] **gaunt** [gɔːnt]: hager; mager – [14] **blotch** [blɔtʃ]: Fleck; Klecks; (*med.*) Ausschlag – [14] **bencvolent** [biˈnevələnt]: wohlwollend; nicht bösartig; harmlos – [15] **cancer** [ˈkænsə]: (*med.*) Krebs – [16] **well:** beträchtlich; ziemlich stark – [22] **Santiago** [sɑnˈtjɑgo] – [23] **to haul up** [hɔːl]: hinaufziehen; hinaufzerren.

[8] **shack** [ʃæk]: Hütte – [11] **gear** [giə]: Gerät; Zubehör; Ausrüstung – 6
[12/13] **budshield** [ˈbʌdʃiːld]: Knospenscheide – [13] **guano** [ˈgwɑːnou]: in Kuba üblicher Sammelbegriff für Palmen – [14] **dirt floor:** Fußboden aus Erde; erdener Fußboden – [15] **charcoal** [ˈtʃɑːkoul]: Holzkohle – [16] **to overlap:** übereinandergreifen; überlappen – [16] **sturdy fibred** [ˈstəːdi ˈfaibəd]: hartfaserig – [18] **Cobre** [ˈkɔbre]: Ort in Kuba – [19] **tinted** [ˈtintid]: koloriert; getönt – [26] **cast net:** Wurfnetz – [29] **fiction:** Dichtung; etwas Erdichtetes – [29] **they went through this fiction every day:** (*etwa*) sie spielten diese Komödie jeden Tag – [32] **the fish dresses out:** der Fisch wiegt ausgenommen – [34] **sardine** [sɑːˈdiːn]: Sardine.

[3] **a terminal of the lottery** [ˈtəːminl]: ein Los der letzten Ziehung – 7
[26] **stew** [stjuː]: Eintopfgericht – [27] **two-decker metal container:** zweistöckiger Metallbehälter – [28] **paper napkin:** Papierserviette – [31] **American League** [liːg]: ein Verband von 10 Baseball-Vereinen, die untereinander Spiele austragen, um die beste Mannschaft zu ermitteln –

[31] **Yankees** ['jæŋkiz]: Name eines New Yorker Baseball-Vereins – [34] **Di Maggio** [di'madʒiou]: berühmter Baseball-Spieler.

8 [5] **Sisler** ['sislə]: berühmter Baseball-Spieler – [7] **to be before the mast:** vor dem Mast fahren – [7/8] **square-rigged ship:** rahgetakeltes Schiff – [13] **Luque** [ljuːk] – [13/14] **Mike Gonzales** ['maik gon'θaleθ] – [18] **Qué va!** (*Span.*): Ach was! – [24] **resolution:** Entschlossenheit; Entschluß – [33] **spring:** Sprungfeder.

9 [3] **to live along:** leben an – [4] **surf** [səːf]: Brandung – [4] **to roar:** tosen, brausen; donnern – [5] **tar** [tɑː]: Teer – [5] **oakum** ['oukəm]: Werg – [11] **dusk:** (Abend-)Dämmerung – [13] **he simply woke:** er wachte einfach auf – [14] **to urinate** ['juərineit]: urinieren – [18] **cot** [kɔt]: leichte Bettstelle; Lager.

10 [1] **condensed-milk cans:** Büchsenmilchdosen; Kondensmilchdosen – [6] **manolin** [mano'lin] – [9] **bait** [beit]: Köder – [24] **pebbled** ['pebld]: mit Kieselsteinen durchsetzt – [24] **pebbled sand:** Kieselsand – [27] **rope lashings:** Tauwerk – [28] **oar** [ɔː]: Ruder; Riemen – [28] **thole pin** [θoul]: Dolle; Vorrichtung zum Halten der Riemen – [29] **thrust:** Druck – [31] **the dip:** das Eintauchen.

11 [7] **the trembling sound:** (*hier*) das Surren – [8] **to hiss:** zischen – [9] **to soar away:** davonsegeln – [11] **tern** [təːn]: Seeschwalbe – [14] **robber birds:** Raubvögel – [15] **sea swallow:** Seeschwalbe – [17] **to dip:** kurz ins Wasser eintauchen – [20/21] **he kept well within his speed:** (*etwa*) er ruderte zügig, ohne sich dabei zu überanstrengen – [22] **swirl:** Wirbel; Strudel – [26] **to work the deep wells:** er durchkämmte die tiefen Fischtanks – [26] **to do nothing:** (*hier*) nichts erreichen, schaffen – [27] **school:** Schwarm; Schule; Zug – [27] **bonito** (*pl.:* bonita) [bo'niːtou]: Blaufisch: ein makrelenartiger Fisch – [28] **albacore** ['ælbəkɔːr]: Albacore: ein Thunfisch – [30] **fathom** ['fæðəm]: Faden: ein Tiefenmaß – [33] **shank** [ʃæŋk]: Schaft – [34] **to project** [prə'dʒekt]: herausragen; herausstehen; vorspringen – [35] **curve:** Bogen – [35] **point:** Spitze.

12 [2] **half-garland** ['hɑːf-'gɑːlənd]: Halbgirlande – [5] **the dip:** das Auf- und Niedertauchen – [11] **far inshore:** dicht vor der Küste – [19] **sifting:** Treiben; Wogen – [20] **plankton** ['plæŋktən] – [24] **stern line:** Achterleine – [24] **taut** [tɔːt]: straff – [25] **loop:** Schlinge; Bucht – [26] **tuna** ['tuːnə]:

Thunfisch – [27] **to commence:** beginnen – [27] **to haul in:** einholen –
[31] **to thump:** schlagen; plumpsen – [32] **planking of the boat:** Bootsplan-
ken – [34] **for kindness:** aus Gutmütigkeit – [35] **shade:** Schatten –
[35] **stern:** Heck.

[6] **smack:** Schmack(e): kleines Küsten- oder Fischerfahrzeug – [10] **to** 13
trickle: rieseln; tröpfeln – [11] **bight:** Bucht (im Tau); Schlinge – [16] **to**
ship the oars: die Ruder einlegen – [16] **to bump:** stoßen – [20] **tentative**
['tentətiv]: Probe- – [21] **marlin** ['mɑːlin]: Marlin (Art Schwertfisch) –
[23] **hand-forged:** handgeschmiedet.

[1] **eat them good** (*coll.*): friß sie tüchtig auf – [20] **reserve coil** [kɔil]: 14
Reserverollen – [23] **imperceptible** [impə'septəbl]: unmerklich – [24] **side-**
ways: seitlich.

[8] **to come up easy:** (*hier*) gemächlich heraufkommen – [13] **alternately** 15
[ɔːl'təːnitli]: abwechselnd – [14] **to pivot** ['pivət]: sich mitdrehen – [20] **to**
brace oneself: sich stützen; sich stemmen – [20] **thwart:** Ruderbank;
Ducht – [26] **to tow:** (ab-)schleppen; ins Schlepptau nehmen – [26] **towing**
bitt: schleppendes Beting; Beting: Gerüst auf Schiffen oder Booten zur
Befestigung der Ankerketten – [31] **to sound:** wegtauchen; auf Grund
gehen – [33] **slant:** Neigung.

[2/3] **he was still braced solidly:** er stand immer noch breitbeinig, mit an- 16
gespannten Muskeln da – [4] **to hook** (a fish): (einen Fisch) fangen –
[8] **Havana** [hə'vænə] – [16/17] **he worked it down under . . .:** er bugsierte
es unter . . . – [21] **tolerable** ['tɔlərəbl]: erträglich.

[12] **when once:** da nun einmal doch – [12] **treachery** ['tretʃəri]: (*hier*) 17
List – [15] **snare:** Schlinge – [24] **gunwale** ['gʌnl]: Dollbord: obere Planke
auf dem Bootsbord – [25] **a sheath knife:** ein in einer Scheide steckendes
Messer – [31] **to sever:** abschneiden; durchschneiden.

[1] **Catalan** ['kætələn]: katalanisch – [1] **cordel** [kɔː'del] (*Sp.*): Schnur; 18
dünner Strick – [2] **leader:** Öse – [5] **broadbill:** Schwertfisch – [5] **shark**
[ʃɑːk]: Hai – [13] **surge:** Woge; Welle – [15] **to coagulate** [kou'ægjuleit]:
gerinnen – [17] **to adjust:** zurechtrücken – [21] **lurch:** Ruck.

[9] **submerged** [səb'məːdʒd]: untergetaucht; unter Wasser – [15] **to brace** 20

oneself: sich abstützen – [16]**line burn:** Wunde, die von einer scheuernden Leine verursacht wurde – [25]**longitudinally** [lɔndʒi'tjuːdinəli]: der Länge nach – [29]**carcass** ['kɑːkəs]: Gerippe.

21 [9]**lime:** Limone – [11]**rigor mortis:** Totenstarre – [17]**dolphin** ['dɔlfin]: Delphin – [34]**to gentle the fingers:** die Finger lockern.

22 [3]**to come back:** (*hier*) wieder in Ordnung kommen – [3]**of one's own accord:** aus eigenem Antrieb; freiwillig – [4]**to abuse** [ə'bjuːz]: übermäßig beanspruchen; mißbrauchen – [8]**hurricane months** ['hʌrikən]: Orkanmonate – [17]**to bulge** [bʌldʒ]: sich (aus-)bauchen; sich wölben – [20]**lavender** ['lævində] – [21]**baseball bat:** Baseballschläger – [21]**tapered** ['teipəd]: spitz zulaufend – [21]**rapier** ['reipjə]: Rapier – [23]**scythe** [saið]: Sense.

23 [5]**eagle** ['iːgl]: Adler.

24 [23]**pectoral fins** ['pektərəl]: Brustflossen – [24]**erect** [i'rekt]: aufgerichtet – [31]**muscle** ['mʌsl]: Muskel.

25 [1]**Sargasso weed** [sɑː'gæsou]: Sargassotang – [9]**to cut:** sich schnell (durch etwas) bewegen – [27]**to gut:** ausnehmen; ausweiden – [29]**drag:** Bremse – [33]**to ease oneself:** es sich bequem machen.

26 [4]**dorado** [do'rɑːdo]: Goldmakrele – [15]**sustenance** ['sʌstinəns]: Nahrung; Ernährung – [19]**Rigel** ['raigəl]: Rigel: ein Stern im Sternbild des Orion – [29]**to relax** [ri'læks]: nachlassen.

27 [2]**drag:** Bremse – [5]**to prolong:** verlängern – [17]**to comprehend** [kɔmpri'hend]: verstehen.

28 [11]**norther:** Nordwind – [24]**to brake:** bremsen.

29 [6]**calloused** ['kæləst]: schwielig – [7]**palm** [pɑːm]: Handfläche – [11]**to stoop down:** sich niederbeugen; sich bücken – [11]**to scoop up:** schöpfen – [13]**to nauseate** ['nɔːsieit]: (jmd.) Übelkeit erregen – [13]**to vomit:** sich übergeben; brechen.

30 [3]**grudgingly** ['grʌdʒiŋli]: widerwillig; ungern – [17]**faint and dizzy:**

schwach und schwindlig – 19 **to fail oneself:** sich selbst aufgeben – 19 **to die on a fish like this:** sterben wegen eines solchen Fisches – 21 **to endure** [in'djuə]: ausharren; durchhalten – 24 **to bang:** schlagen – 24 **to jerk** [dʒəːk]: rucken – 26 **wire leader:** Drahtöse – 26 **spear:** Speer – 28 **I would rather:** es wäre mir lieber.

9 **bow** [bau]: Bug – 11 **to work on somebody:** jemanden bearbeiten – 31
14 **to recover line:** Leine wiedereinholen – 17 **the weaving pulling:** (*etwa*) das schwingende Ziehen – 19 **trade wind:** Passatwind.

3 **to rake back** [reik]: (*hier*) zurückfallen – 4 **bulk:** große, massige Ge- 32
stalt; massiger Körper; großer Umfang – 5 **dorsal fin** ['dɔːsəl]: Rükkenflosse – 6 **pectorals** ['pektərəlz]: Brustflossen – 8 **sucking fish:** Saugfisch – 9 **to dart off:** davonsausen; davonschießen – 12 **eel** [iːl]: Aal – 14 **placid** ['plæsid]: gelassen; ruhig – 24 **to rig:** (auf-)montieren – 25 **bitt:** Beting.

3 **to start it well out before ...:** es beginnen lange bevor ... – 5 **to right** 33
oneself: sich aufrichten – 9 **to accomplish** [ə'kɔmpliʃ]: erreichen – 33 **mushy:** zerschunden; breiig.

4 **bill:** Schnabel; schnabelähnliche Schnauze – 6 **interminable** [in'təː- 34
minəbl]: grenzenlos; endlos – 9 **to summon:** zusammenraffen; aufbieten – 10 **chest fin** [tʃest]: Brustflosse – 11 **altitude** ['æltitjuːd]: Höhe – 13 **to come alive:** lebendig werden – 21 **shaft** [ʃaːft]: Schaft – 24 **shoal** [ʃoul]: Untiefe – 27 **glimpse:** flüchtiger Blick; glimpse of a vision: flüchtige Vision – 33 **noose:** Schlinge – 33 **to lash:** festbinden; festmachen – 34 **to swamp** ['swɔmp]: voll Wasser laufen lassen (beim Laden) – 35 **to bail out:** ausschöpfen.

17 **to splice:** spleißen: Tauenden miteinander verflechten – 19 **to wallow:** 35
sich wälzen – 23 **gill** [gil]: Kieme – 27 **to go astern** [əs'təːn]: achtern gehen – 27 **to noose:** anschlingen – 31 **detached:** objektiv; distanziert; entrückt – 31 **periscope** ['periskoup]: Sehrohr; Beobachtungsspiegel.

1 **the fish dresses out:** der Fisch wiegt ausgenommen – 5/6 **middle** 36
thwart: mittlere Ruderbank – 9 **to step the mast:** den Mast aufrichten – 10 **boom:** Spiere; Stange am Segel – 10 **to rig:** auftakeln – 14 **he only needed the feel of the trade wind:** er brauchte nur den Passatwind zu

spüren – 15 **spoon**(-bait)**:** Blinker; Löffelköder – 19 **shrimp:** Garnele – 21 **sand flea:** Sandfloh – 21 **to pinch off:** abkneifen.

37 4 **cumulus** ['kjuːmjuləs] – 5 **cirrus** ['sirəs] – 18 **Mako shark:** Makohai – 20 **swordfish:** Schwertfisch – 24 **to waver:** schwanken – 28 **to be crisped:** gekräuselt sein; (*hier*) zusammengekrallt sein – 30 **to feed on:** sich nähren von.

38 10 **to close astern:** sich nähern von achtern – 12 **chop** [tʃɔp]**:** Hieb; Schlag; (*hier*) Zuschnappen – 16 **to intersect with:** sich schneiden, kreuzen mit – 19/20 **location:** Lage; Sitz – 22 **malignancy** [mə'lignənsi]**:** Feindseligkeit – 30 **to come taut:** (= to become taut) sich straffen – 30 **to snap:** reißen.

39 2 **to mutilate** ['mjuːtileit]**:** verstümmeln – 21 **butt:** (dickes) Ende; (*hier*) Griff – 23 **tiller:** Ruderpinne – 23 **sheet:** Schot; Segelleine.

40 13 **scavenger** ['skævindʒə]**:** Aasfresser – 24 **stringiness:** Zähigkeit – 28 **to back into:** sich drehen nach – 29 **to fall off:** abflauen – 31 **hull:** Rumpf (eines Schiffes).

41 7/8 **shovel-nosed shark** ['ʃʌvl-nouzd]**:** schaufelnasiger Hai – 13 **to jam:** (ein-)klemmen; (ein-)zwängen – 18 **to flinch:** zurückschrecken; kneifen; (*hier*) zurückzucken – 23 **turtle** ['təːtl]**:** Schildkröte – 23 **flipper:** (Schwimm-)Flosse – 26 **slime:** Schleim – 34/35 **spinal cord** ['spainl kɔːd]**:** Rückenmark – 35 **juncture** ['dʒʌŋktʃə]**:** Verbindungsstelle.

42 6 **to swing broadside:** quer schwingen – 17 **vertebrae** ['vəːtibriː] (*pl.*)**:** Wirbelsäule – 17 **brain:** (*hier*) Schädeldecke – 18 **cartilage** ['kɑːtilidʒ]**:** Knorpel – 18 **to sever** ['sevə]**:** sich trennen; sich spalten; (zer-)reißen – 18 **to reverse** [ri'vəːs]**:** umdrehen – 28 **to drain:** entwässern; drained of blood: ausgeblutet – 29 **awash** [ə'wɔʃ]**:** ausgewaschen; gewässert.

43 26 **trough** [trɔf]**:** Trog – 35 **club:** Keule.

44 11 **to quarter on:** stöbern nach; durchstöbern – 12 **scent:** (*hier*) Witterung – 12 **to head for:** lossteuern auf; losgehen auf – 18 **to flex:** biegen; beugen; (*hier*) zufassen.

[6] **sluggishly:** schwerfällig; träge – [10] **in my time:** in meinen besten Jahren – [33] **hatchet** [ˈhætʃit]: Axt. 45

[34] **perceptible** [pəˈseptəbl]: wahrnehmbar. 46

[6] **sore** [sɔː]: wund – [12] **phosphorescence** [fɔsfəˈresns]: Leuchten – [32] **coppery:** kupferfarbig. 47

[2] **jagged** [ˈdʒægid]: zersplittert; zerfetzt – [27] **patch:** Fleck; Stück – [27] **shingle:** (*hier*) steiniger Strand – [31] **to unstep:** herunternehmen. 48

[12] **lance** [lɑːns]: Speer – [13] **spring leaf:** Blattfeder – [15] **to temper:** härten – [34] **coral rock:** Korallenfels. 51

[3] **barracuda** [bærəˈkuːdə]: Barracuda; Pfeilhecht – [8] **garbage** [ˈgɑːbidʒ]: Abfall – [10] **tiburon** [tibuˈrɔn]: Sammelbegriff für alle Haifischarten – [10] **Eshark:** ’n Hai. 52